How *Wicked* Made It to the Stage

Jeri Freedman

Cavendish Square

New York

Published in 2019 by Cavendish Square Publishing, LLC
243 5th Avenue, Suite 136, New York, NY 10016

First Edition

Website: cavendishsq.com

This publication represents the opinions and views of the author based on his or
her personal experience, knowledge, and research. The information in this book
serves as a general guide only. The author and publisher have used their best
efforts in preparing this book and disclaim liability rising directly or
indirectly from the use and application of this book.

All websites were available and accurate when this book was sent to press.

Library of Congress Cataloging-in-Publication Data

Names: Freedman, Jeri, author.
Title: How Wicked Made it to the Stage / Jeri Freedman.
Description: New York : Cavendish Square, [2018] | Series: Getting to
Broadway | Includes bibliographical references and index.
Identifiers: LCCN 2017058840 (print) | LCCN 2017059322 (ebook) | ISBN
9781502635150 (e-Book) | ISBN 9781502635143 (library bound : alk. paper) |
ISBN 9781502635167 (pbk. : alk. paper)
Subjects: LCSH: Schwartz, Stephen. Wicked--Juvenile literature.
Classification: LCC ML3930.S394 (ebook) |
LCC ML3930.S394 F74 2018 (print) | DDC 792.6/42--dc23
LC record available at https://lccn.loc.gov/2017058840

Editorial Director: David McNamara
Editor: Tracey Maciejewski
Copy Editor: Rebecca Rohan
Associate Art Director: Amy Greenan
Designer: Lindsey Auten
Production Coordinator: Karol Szymczuk
Photo Research: J8 Media

Printed in the United States of America

Contents

CHAPTER 1 ... Roots in Oz   5

CHAPTER 2 ... The Yellow Brick Road
to Broadway   21

CHAPTER 3 ... Reaching the Great White Way   45

CHAPTER 4 ... *Wicked* Influence   69

Glossary   83

Further Information   86

Bibliography   89

Index   94

About the Author   96

Roots in Oz

The musical *Wicked* opened on Broadway in October 2003 and became the epitome of spectacular musical theater. The show has run for more than thirteen years and is still going strong. It has grossed over one billion dollars, largely due to its appeal to women and girls, who have embraced the message of the main character: Elphaba, the Wicked Witch of the West, a misfit who discovers her inner strength and power. It is this fact that has made it the eighth longest-running Broadway musical, according to *Playbill* magazine, and it is likely to continue to climb up the rankings.

Wicked the Novel

The musical is based on the 1995 novel *Wicked: The Life and Times of the Wicked Witch of the West* by Gregory Maguire. Unlike the original *The Wonderful Wizard of Oz* by L. Frank Baum, *Wicked* is not a children's book. Maguire

Opposite: Elphaba, the misunderstood Wicked Witch of the West in *Wicked*

was a writer of children's books before he embarked on *Wicked*, but *Wicked* is an adult novel with a dark, gritty, mature tone, containing a great deal of sexual and political material. In a *New York Times* article, "Mr. Wicked," journalist Alex Mitchel recounts the story of Maguire standing in the lobby of the Gershwin Theatre, where the musical version of *Wicked* is performed. He was telling the mothers of nine-, ten-, and thirteen-year-olds that the girls shouldn't read the novel *Wicked* until their freshman year in college. In response to their crestfallen looks, he amended his recommendation to say that if their mothers read it first and thought reading it was okay, they could do so at 16.

The novel, which takes place in Oz in the years before Dorothy's arrival, explores political, social, and ethical issues. From the time he was young, Maguire had difficulties with such issues in Baum's *The Wonderful Wizard of Oz*. For instance, he questioned whether it was right for the Wizard to command Dorothy to kill the Wicked Witch of the West just because she was wicked. (One could make a case that he was merely trying to get Dorothy out of his hair by having the witch kill her, so his deceptions wouldn't be exposed, but that isn't exactly a moral position either.)

In Maguire's version of Oz, a green girl named Elphaba Thropp is born in Munchkinland. Her parents are a Unionist minister named Frex and his dissatisfied, alcoholic wife, Melena. Elphaba is intelligent but is an outcast because of her green skin. A mysterious stranger was spending time with her mother prior to her becoming pregnant and gave her a mysterious green potion. There is a suggestion that this stranger is Elphaba's real father. During her childhood, the Wizard arrives and assumes control of Oz. Her mother gives birth to a second daughter, Nessarose, who is pink but lacks arms. The book moves on to Elphaba's years at Shiz University, where she rooms with the social-climbing Galinda (who later changes her name to Glinda), and is harassed by the manipulative and dangerous headmistress, Madame Morrible. She becomes involved in the animal rights movement, in this case representing sentient animals (those who act much like human beings). Elphaba and Galinda travel to the Emerald City and see the Wizard about the plight of the animals. When the Wizard dismisses the issue out of hand, Galinda leaves the city, but Elphaba stays and works with a secret group to overthrow the Wizard. Elphaba begins to practice magic. Nessarose, also a practicing witch, becomes the ruler of Munchkinland. She is killed when Dorothy's house falls on her during a tornado. When Elphaba returns for the funeral, she encounters Glinda, who is now also a witch. They part on unfriendly terms after arguing about politics and the fact that Glinda has given Nessarose's shoes to Dorothy. Elphaba meets with the Wizard and discovers that not only is he from another world, but he's probably her real father. The Wizard sends Dorothy and the companions traveling with her to kill Elphaba. Dorothy tries to apologize to Elphaba for killing Nessarose, but the meeting results in an angry confrontation during which Elphaba's broom catches fire and she accidently sets the house alight. Dorothy, attempting to put out the blaze, tosses water on

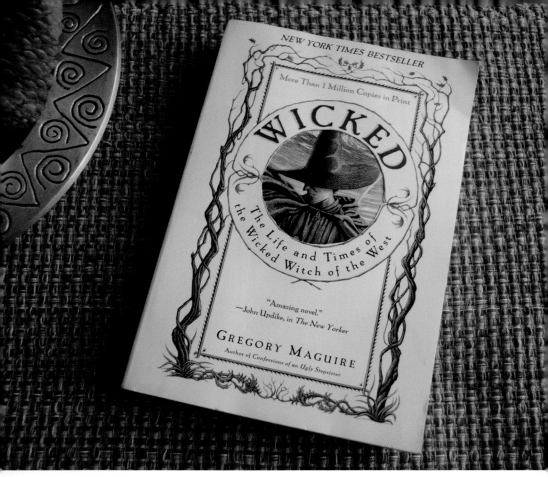

Gregory Maguire's original novel on which the musical *Wicked* is based

Elphaba, which kills her. Across Oz, Elphaba is recalled as
the Wicked Witch of the West.

Maguire had the idea of writing *Wicked* when he was
living in London in the 1990s, near the time the Gulf War
started. He read a headline comparing Saddam Hussein to
Hitler. The mere mention of Hitler evoked a sense of evil.
Several months later, the British press covered the murder
of a toddler by a group of schoolboys. These incidents led
him to wonder whether one could be born evil. He was

also troubled by the human tendency to paint those who oppose their views as "evil." He decided to use an iconic evil character in American culture, the Wicked Witch of the West, to explore these questions. In the "Mr. Wicked" article, Maguire is quoted as saying, "I wanted to write about the nature of evil and the various ways in which people demonize their enemies." After he began to consider the witch in the context of how people bully others, he started to wonder what he really knew about her, beside the fact that the Wizard tells Dorothy the witch is very wicked, then sends her and her friends to kill this wicked witch. Maguire was also influenced by the fact that he had lived his life in the shadow of the Vietnam War, fearing he would be drafted and sent off to kill "wicked" Vietcong. He felt that, like Nixon, the Wizard of Oz was sending "innocent foot soldiers" to kill others—something he wasn't willing to do himself. (The military draft ended a week before Maguire would have been eligible.)

Facts You May Not Know

WHY ELPHABA?
L. Frank Baum never gives the name of the Wicked Witch of the West in *The Wonderful Wizard of Oz*. It was Maguire who named her Elphaba, using Baum's initials, LFB, as the basis of her name.

In many cases, once the producer of a play options the rights to material on which a play is based, the author of the original material has little say in how the play is produced.

This was not the case with *Wicked*, however. Maguire approved the three individuals primarily responsible for creating the show: the composer and lyricist Stephen Schwartz, the book writer Winnie Holzman, and the director, Joe Mantello.

Oz in the Media

Wicked is far from the first show based on *The Wonderful Wizard of Oz*. Nor was it the first revisionist version of the story. There have been numerous stage, film, and televised versions, the latter both live-action and animated. Some productions stuck close to Baum's story; others presented alternative versions of Oz or original sequels, such as NBC's short-lived 2016–2017 TV series *Emerald City*, a dark, modern reimagining of Baum's Oz.

In fact, the first stage version of the book was created by L. Frank Baum himself. Baum loved the theater. In 1901, at the same time as the publication of *The Wonderful Wizard of Oz*, Baum started planning a stage version, along with illustrator W. W. Denslow and Paul Tietjens, a twenty-four-year-old composer. Baum wrote the book (story and dialogue) for the play, closely mirroring the story in his book, as well as the lyrics, for which Tietjens wrote the music. Denslow worked on the physical design. Fred Hamlin, producer of the Grand Opera House in Chicago, agreed to produce the play, and it was directed by Julian Mitchell. Mitchell knew what was likely to be successful in the theater and made changes to the script and songs. When the show opened in the summer of 1902, it was a hit. Mitchell made plans to take the show to Broadway. He brought in another writer, Glen Macdonough, to create a different third act, and songs were changed or cut. *The Wizard of Oz* opened on Broadway in January 1903 at the Majestic Theatre. At first, Baum was angered by the changes Mitchell had made, but when the show became a hit on Broadway, that anger was alleviated.

Most people are familiar with the 1939 movie, *The Wizard of Oz*, produced by the Metro-Goldwyn-Meyer (MGM) film studio and starring Judy Garland as Dorothy. Like *Wicked*, the film version of *The Wizard of Oz* was a musical. The film does vary from Baum's book in some ways. Because of time constraints, many of the details included in the book, such as the backstories of the Scarecrow, Cowardly Lion, and Tin Woodman, were left out, and the film omits the Good Witch of the North entirely. In other places, Baum's story was changed in ways that make it lighter than the book. However, it does keep the general personalities of the characters—for example, the Wicked Witch of the West is still wicked.

Another musical based on *The Wonderful Wizard of Oz* opened at the Morris A. Mechanic Theatre in Baltimore, Maryland, in 1974, and moved to Broadway in 1975. *The Wiz* featured an all-black cast and used Baum's story to capture the black experience in an urban setting. In taking this approach, it anticipated Maguire's use of the story to explore political and social themes. The show won seven Tony Awards, including Best Musical. A film version of *The Wiz* was produced by Universal Studios and Motown

THE ORIGINAL WIZARD OF OZ

There would be no *Wicked*, or Wicked Witch of the West, if it weren't for *The Wonderful Wizard of Oz*, written by L. Frank Baum and illustrated by W. W. Denslow. The book was originally published by the George M. Hill Company of Chicago in 1900. In a 1903 *Publishers Weekly* interview, Baum said the name Oz came from a file cabinet he had labeled O–Z. Before becoming a successful writer, Baum had unsuccessfully tried many jobs to support his family: an actor, an axle oil salesman, a journalist, a chicken breeder, a variety store owner, and a china salesman.

Baum drew on his own environment and experiences in writing the book.

A 2000 article in the *Chicago Tribune* notes that as a boy, Baum often had nightmares of a scarecrow chasing him across a field, only to collapse at the last moment. According to Baum's son Harry, his father was fascinated with window displays. The same year he published *The Wonderful Wizard of Oz*, he published *The Art of Decorating Dry Goods Windows and Interiors*, and for three years he was the editor of *The Show Window: A Journal of Practical Window Trimming for the Merchant and the Professional*. His son Harry recalls that his father wished to make something captivating for a window display in his variety store, so he made a figure from scrap parts, using a wash boiler for the body, stovepipes bolted on for limbs, a saucepan for a face, and a funnel for a hat. Harry says this tin mannequin became the Tin Woodman. According to Evan Schwartz, author of the book *Finding Oz: How L. Frank Baum Discovered the*

Great American Story, the inspiration for the yellow brick road might have come from the roads of Peekskill, New York, a town Baum lived near when he was young. Its roads were paved with yellow bricks imported from Holland. Schwartz and other scholars also suggest that the idea for the Emerald City might have been inspired by the majestic complex of the Columbia Exhibition of 1893, better known as the Chicago World's Fair.

The original version of *The Wonderful Wizard of Oz* by L. Frank Baum

In creating *The Wonderful Wizard of Oz*, Baum was inspired by another great work of children's literature, Lewis Carroll's *Alice's Adventures in Wonderland*. Baum noted that a major reason Carroll's book was so popular was that its central character was a child with whom the audience could identify. Baum agreed with Carroll's view that children's books should be enjoyable to read and not loaded with moral lessons, as was common at the time. Baum wanted to create a children's book with engaging fantasy elements, but he also wanted to incorporate uniquely American elements in the story. In the introduction to *The Wonderful Wizard of Oz*, Baum stated that "it aspires to being a modernized fairy tale, in which the wonderment and joy are retained and the heartaches and nightmares are left out." This goal is in marked contrast to Maguire's approach in *Wicked*, which is to take the fairytale characters and treat them as if they were in a reality-based world with all the conflicts and problems of real people.

Productions, starring Michael Jackson as the Scarecrow and Richard Pryor as the Wizard. *The Wiz Live!*, a live broadcast of the stage version of the musical, aired on NBC in December 2015.

In 2013, Disney produced its own revisionist version of *The Wonderful Wizard of Oz* in the film *Oz the Great and Powerful*, directed by Sam Raimi and written by David Lindsay-Abaire and Mitchell Kapner. The film takes place twenty years before the events in the original novel. It tells the story of Oscar Diggs, a duplicitous stage magician who is enlisted by the people of Oz to restore order and resolve the conflicts between three witches: Theodora, Evanora, and Glinda. The film features a number of touches that harken back to the 1939 MGM film *The Wizard of Oz*, including an opening sequence in black and white that switches to color in Oz and a song by the Munchkins that, to some extent, parodies "The Munchkinland Song" in the MGM film. Warner Brothers, which bought MGM's film library in 1986, owns the rights to the original movie. Warner threatened to sue Disney if they infringed on the MGM version, including using the color green for the Wicked Witch, as in the 1939 film. Therefore, Disney made a determined effort not to do anything that could be construed as taken from the MGM film. For example, Glinda is referred to by her title in Baum's book, the Good Witch of the South, and an assortment of races other than the Munchkins are included, such as the Quadlings, the china doll inhabitants of Dainty China Country, and the Winkies—who are all found in Baum's work. In the film, the witch Theodora's tears leave streaks

The main cast of *The Wiz*, the musical based on the Wizard of Oz

of scars on her face, reflecting her weakness to water in the original novel/film. Also, as in Baum's story, Oz is presented as a real place, not as a dream from which Dorothy awakes in the 1939 film. Kapner had long wanted to write a prequel to the 1939 film, but he couldn't find support for his project until after *Wicked* became successful. Although the film is presented as a prequel whose purpose is to explain how the Wizard came to rule Oz, it is also an attempt to present an

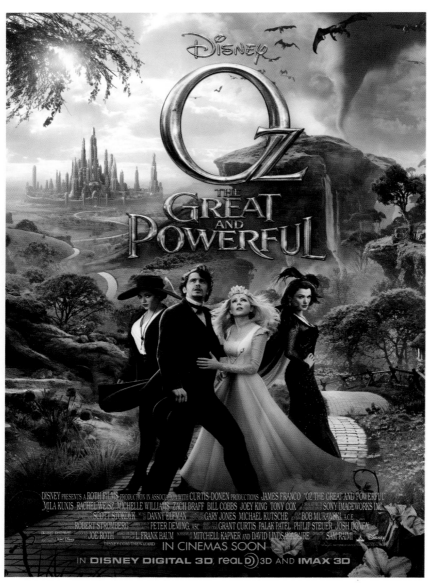

A poster captures Disney's 2013 vision for the movie *Oz the Great and Powerful.*

alternate version of Baum's story from the point of view of the Wizard, just as *Wicked* is a version of the story from the Wicked Witch's point of view. It is hard to escape the suspicion that the tremendous success of the musical *Wicked* contributed to the idea of making a version of the story from another character's viewpoint.

The Beginning of the Road

Shortly after Maguire's novel was published, the film production company headed by actress/producer Demi Moore optioned the film rights in conjunction with Universal Studios. The production company worked on a screenplay for three years, but they couldn't come up with a version that Marc Platt, the producer for Universal, found acceptable.

In 1996, composer/ lyricist Stephen Schwartz was on vacation in Hawaii with friend and fellow songwriter John Bucchino, who was providing musical accompaniment for folksinger Holly Near. Near mentioned to Schwartz that

Composer and lyricist Stephen Schwartz in the 1990s, when he was working on *Wicked*

she was reading the novel *Wicked* and explained what the story was about. Schwartz was captivated by the idea of a stage musical of the prequel to *The Wonderful Wizard of Oz*, and especially by the main character, Elphaba. He felt that she had the potential to be a powerful focus for the play, around whom big musical numbers could be staged. He also recognized that many people would relate to her feeling of being a misfit and would identify with her. Upon his return to his home in Los Angeles, Schwartz had his lawyer make inquiries about the rights to make a stage musical from the book, and he learned that Demi Moore's production company and Universal had control of the rights.

Schwartz wasn't the only one with an interest in obtaining the rights, however. Writer Winnie Holzman, who ultimately wrote the book (the non-musical parts) for *Wicked*, had also discovered Maguire's novel, and she thought it would make a great screenplay. Like Schwartz, she found that Demi Moore and Universal had the rights, but once she found that Universal was already working on a screenplay, she gave up on her idea of doing one.

Schwartz was reluctant to give up his idea of turning the novel into a play. In 1997, he met with Platt and tried to convince him to give up on the idea of making a movie version of *Wicked* and let him produce it as a theatrical musical. Platt was not convinced to abandon his plans for a film, but his discussion with Schwartz made him realize that making the show a musical was exactly what was needed to make it work. He thought songs would make the story come alive for three reasons: (1) The idea of Oz as a musical had already been established by the 1939 MGM musical. (2) Music can heighten the feeling of fantasy in an imaginary world. (3) Songs would allow the characters to communicate their thoughts and feelings to the audience directly. In a novel, the author can simply tell the reader what's going on in the characters' minds, but it's hard to do this visually in a movie. In a musical, however, characters can sing about what they are feeling, connecting to the audience and affecting them emotionally. Ultimately, Schwartz convinced Platt to embark on developing *Wicked* with him first as a musical stage play, with the idea of doing a movie version later.

Chapter 2

The Yellow Brick Road to Broadway

Stephen Schwartz suggested to Marc Platt that Winnie Holzman be the book writer for the musical version of *Wicked*. Aside from her experience in theatrical book writing, she had written for television, and Platt was familiar with her work on shows such as *My So-Called Life*. Platt agreed that Holzman would be a good choice. However, before they could go forward with their plans, they needed the approval of Gregory Maguire.

In November 1998, Schwartz called Maguire and arranged to meet with him. Schwartz explained that the novel would translate well to a musical. One reason for

Opposite: Gregory Maguire, author of the novel *Wicked*, at the Los Angeles premiere of the musical

this was that it contained strong emotions that could be effectively turned into songs. Maguire let Schwartz try to win him over to the idea, but he actually loved musical theater, and he was familiar with Schwartz's work on the musicals *Godspell* and *Pippin*. Maguire was well aware that presenting the story on stage would mean changes, and it might become more of a comedy-drama. However, he decided that as long as the "fundamental questions explored in the book were carried through," he could accept that. Maguire agreed to the project.

The Music of Oz

Schwartz started writing ideas and possible song lines in a spiral notebook. Creating the musical version of *Wicked* would not be easy—he needed to turn a 405-page novel into one evening at the theater. In his novel, Maguire had left hints that some of the events in his story had led to the version of Oz in Baum's *The Wonderful Wizard of Oz*, but he hadn't explicitly explained these relationships. Schwartz used some of these "hooks" as subplots in his stage version. He incorporated the seeds of the backstories of the Scarecrow, Tin Woodman, and Cowardly Lion, for example. He conceived of *Wicked* as following the precedent set by the musicals *Annie* and *Gypsy*, which presented the early lives of characters before they became the figures the public knows. For instance, *Annie* tells the story of how Daddy Warbucks and Annie met prior to the events that take place in the comic strip. This approach provides a natural show-stopping moment when the character in the play develops

Stephen Schwartz at work. Composing the songs required many changes along the way.

into the character the audience knows. There are thirty-eight major and supporting characters in Maguire's book, far too many for a stage musical. Schwartz had to select the ones he wanted to focus on. In the book, one of the central conflicts occurs between the Wizard and the intelligent talking animals of Oz, personified by a goat-professor, Dr. Dillamond, who teaches at Shiz University. Schwartz wanted to use the attempts of the Wizard to oppress the Animals (Maguire uses a capital A to differentiate sentient animals from ordinary ones) to reflect how real-world political actions oppress people.

The Yellow Brick Road to Broadway   **23**

By September 1998, he had a total vision for the show and used his notes to create an outline of the performance as he conceived it. He was well aware that the structure would change as he discussed his concepts with Platt and Holzman, but he had a coherent overview that would provide a starting point for constructing the play. Three key elements of his vision were: (1) The show would open with the people of Oz celebrating the death of the Wicked Witch and then switch to flashbacks to tell Elphaba's story. (2) At the end of Act I, Elphaba would come into her power and fly. (3) He didn't want the Wicked Witch to die at the end as she does in Maguire's book and the MGM movie. Although every aspect of the script changed over the period Schwartz and Holzman worked on it, these three elements remained constant.

One of the issues that the collaborators had to work out was the different visions they had for the play. Schwartz believed the show should focus on one central character—Elphaba. Winnie Holzman, in contrast, thought that a love triangle between Glinda, Elphaba, and Prince Fiyero should be a central feature. This love triangle was one example of the ways in which the play differed from the novel, in which Fiyero is married and has an affair with Elphaba. In the play, Fiyero is involved with Elphaba's friend Glinda, and Elphaba's affair with Fiyero represents a deep betrayal, which both adds drama to the story and shows Elphaba's ability to do things that are wicked. Schwartz and Holzman thought it was important to show that Elphaba could do something bad to give her depth as a character, rather than present her as just a misunderstood good girl. Other changes were made for practical rather than philosophical reasons. For example, in Maguire's novel, Elphaba's sister Nessarose is born armless, but for the stage version she is in a wheelchair instead.

Developing the Play

Initially, Schwartz, Holzman, and Platt met in Platt's office, where they worked out the plot of the play scene by scene, using the movie-plotting technique called storyboarding. In this process, a representation of each scene or a one-line description is drawn or written on a card, and the cards can then be arranged on something like a table or a bulletin board. Initially, the team used index cards, writing a brief description of each significant moment in the plot, which they arranged on a large foam board. This method allowed them to change, rearrange, delete, or add elements easily. They spent about a year at the task. When the plot and characters were decided upon, Schwartz and Holzman turned their attention to the songs and script, respectively.

According to Schwartz, as quoted in his biography *Defying Gravity*, when he writes the score for a show, he begins with the song that comes to him most naturally. He says, "Often it's trying to get at the emotional or philosophical center of the story … but not always. It's most important to just open the door and step into the show somewhere." Schwartz begins his songwriting process by coming up with the title for the song, which captures the essence of the song. At first, in keeping with the "good versus wicked" idea, Schwartz thought of incorporating

Stephen Schwartz was born in New York City in 1948 and grew up in Roslyn Heights on Long Island. While in school, he attended the preparatory division of the Juilliard School of Music on weekends, studying piano and composition. He attended Carnegie Mellon University, where he participated in the writing and production of four musicals, including his first version of the musical *Pippin*, which later became a hit on Broadway. He graduated in 1968 with a BFA in drama. After graduating, he worked as a producer for RCA records in New York City but soon began to work on Broadway shows. His first major song used in a Broadway show was "Butterflies Are Free," in 1969 for the play (and later the movie) of the same name.

In 1971, John-Michael Tebelak's *Godspell* played at Café La Mama in New York City for two weeks. It was one of the plays Schwartz had worked on at Carnegie Mellon. The producers, Edgar Lansbury and Joseph Beruh, employed Schwartz to replace most of the songs in the show with new ones. The show opened Off-Broadway at the Cherry Lane Theatre in May 1971 and moved to the Promenade Theatre three months later, then moved again in 1976—this time to Broadway. In 1972, *Pippin* opened on Broadway with Schwartz's music and Bob Fosse directing and choreographing.

In the mid-1990s, Schwartz switched his attention to Hollywood, where he worked as a lyricist with composer Alan Menken on two animated features for Disney, *Pocahontas* in 1995 and *The Hunchback of Notre Dame* in 1996. He then worked on *The Prince of Egypt* for DreamWorks

Animation in 1998 before returning to Broadway in 2003 with *Wicked*.

A scene from *Pippin*, an earlier musical by Stephen Schwartz

Schwartz is a member of the board of directors of the American Society of Composers, Authors, and Publishers (ASCAP), the music industry union. Under the auspices of the ASCAP Foundation, he runs musical theater workshops in New York and Los Angeles. He is also a member of the Council of the Dramatists' Guild, the union for playwrights. He received the Richard Rodgers Award for Excellence in Musical Theater in 2009 and was inducted into the Songwriters Hall of Fame the same year. He has won three Drama Desk awards, two for *Pippin* and one for *Wicked*; four Grammy awards for *Godspell*, *Pocahontas*, *Enchanted*, and *Wicked*; three Academy Awards (Oscars), two for *Pocahontas* and one for *The Prince of Egypt*; a Golden Globe award for *Pocahontas*; and a special Tony award, the Isabelle Stephenson Award, which is given for work with humanitarian, social service, or charitable organizations. He has a star on the Hollywood Walk of Fame.

This picture illustrates a version of storyboarding that uses cards containing elements of a script.

"good," "bad," or a synonym of one of these words into every song title, such as "No One Mourns the Wicked," or "Making Good." However, he soon abandoned this idea as too limiting. He also entertained the idea of composing music for his songs that sounded "otherworldly," with a unique sound that came from Oz, not Earth. When he was unable to develop a scale system of harmonization that did not become tiresome or too bizarre for continuous use, he abandoned the idea. He decided instead to use different musical styles for the songs but incorporate recurring musical themes to unify them. This method is often used in scores, for example, by giving each character a particular musical theme called a leitmotif.

Meanwhile in LA

While Schwartz worked on the score in New York, in Los Angeles, Winnie Holzman wrote the first draft of the book. The two conversed via phone and email to keep the text and songs coordinated. In a 2004 *Playbill* interview, Holzman says of working on *Wicked*, Schwartz "tried to warn me how intense it would be. I thought I was listening, but you never really listen to someone trying to warn you. You have to live it yourself."

One of Holzman's original contributions to the world of *Wicked* was "Oz speak, which consisted of made-up versions of words used in the land of Oz—as opposed to the land of America. Examples of such words are "moodified," "linguification," and "rejoicify."

In 2000, the collaborators began to share information about the *Wicked* project with the public. Stephen Schwartz provided updates about the project in the monthly newsletter published by a website for his fans. While they were developing the script and trying to distill the massive amount of material into a coherent play, Schwartz and

Facts You May Not Know

ECHO OF THE RAINBOW
When Schwartz wrote Elphaba's "Unlimited Theme," he started with the first seven notes of "Somewhere Over the Rainbow" as a homage to songwriter Harold Arlen who wrote the score for MGM's *The Wizard of Oz*. Using eight notes would have qualified as plagiarism.

WINNIE
HOLZMAN

Winnie Holzman was born in Manhattan and grew up in Roslyn Heights, New York, on Long Island. When she was thirteen, she studied at the Circle in the Square Theatre School in New York City. She attended Princeton University in New Jersey and graduated with a degree in English. Holzman received various awards for her poetry, including the Academy of American Poets Prize and the Ward Prize. After graduating, she settled in New York City, where she studied acting.

Holzman performed in comedy sketches, but this didn't provide much in the way of income. She enrolled in the musical theater program at New York University, where she studied with such musical theater greats as Arthur Laurents (*Gypsy*, *West Side Story*), Stephen Sondheim (*A Little Night Music*, *Company*, and *Into the Woods*), Betty Comden and Adolph Green (*Applause*), and Leonard Bernstein (*West Side Story*). She graduated with a master's degree in musical theater writing.

Despite studying musical theater, Holzman began her writing career in television. Holzman's brother, Ernest Holzman, is a cinematographer. Holzman visited him while he was shooting on the set of the TV series *thirtysomething*. While she was there, writer Richard Kramer suggested she should write for the show, and she became a staff writer in 1989. Nine of the episodes in the show's last two seasons were written by Holzman. When the producers of *thirtysomething* went on to produce the TV series *My So-Called Life*, Holzman went to work on that show as well. She started as a story editor, became executive story editor, and ultimately a writer of the series.

TV writer Winnie Holzman created the "book" for *Wicked*.

Beginning in 1998, Holzman worked on *Wicked* while continuing her television work. With her daughter, Savannah, she wrote a pilot for a television series, *Huge* (based on Sasha Paley's novel of the same name) for ABC Family in 2010. The show ran from January to October 2010. From 2014 to 2016, Holzman was a producer and writer for the Showtime television series *Roadies*, a comedy about people working with a touring rock band. Holzman won the Drama Desk Award for Outstanding Book of a Musical and was nominated for the Tony Award for Best Book of a Musical, both for *Wicked*.

Holzman asked playwright Arthur Laurents to read the draft of their script. Laurents, who had been one of Holzman's teachers in college, was the book writer for musicals such as *Gypsy* and *West Side Story*, and a screenwriter, whose movies included *Bonjour Tristesse* and *The Way We Were*. Much to their disappointment, Laurents found the script confusing. He felt it wasn't clear who or what was the focus of the play. Their conversation with Laurents brought out a variety of issues, which they were subsequently able to address. Because the book was so long and had so many subplots, it was difficult to adapt for the stage. For example, there is an entire subplot in the book about the talking Animals. Schwartz and Holzman didn't want to go into the subject in great detail, but it was so central to the story that it had to be included in some form.

Workshopping

At that point, Platt had started his own production company, but it was based in facilities on the Universal lot. He arranged rehearsal space for them at Universal, and in September 2000, they spent two weeks rehearsing. According to Winnie Holzman, the play was too long, and the plot seemed confusing. For the first time, they had an actress, Kristin Chenoweth, to read the role of Glinda.

Schwartz knew Chenoweth's previous work, and Schwartz wanted to cast her in the role. Chenoweth was doing a television sitcom, *Kristin*, in Los Angeles at the time, and she was reluctant to take on another project. However, after she read the script, she decided she really wanted to do the part and joined the reading process. At first, the play was solely about Elphaba, and Glinda was simply a supporting character. However, the charismatic Chenoweth, who had won a Tony in 1999 for *You're a Good Man, Charlie Brown*, brought a new dynamic to the play. Holzman realized she wanted to focus on the friendship between Elphaba and Glinda, but it was impossible to incorporate all of the book's possible subplots. For the audience to follow the story, the play needed a single focal point, and once Winnie decided to have the play revolve around the relationship between Glinda and Elphaba, it started to come together. Stephanie J. Block was recruited to play Elphaba in the readings. (She would later play the same role in the first national tour of *Wicked*.) Block, who was fond of *The Wizard of Oz* story, was captivated by the idea of telling the story from the perspective of the interaction between Elphaba and Glinda. In the wake of this new insight, Holzman rewrote the script.

Kristin Chenoweth (Glinda) at the Broadway premiere of *Wicked* in 2003

Friends of the creative team composed the audience for the first reading of the script at Universal. The actors simply sat at a table and read their parts, while Schwartz played the music for the songs on a piano. The audience responded positively in general, but when Schwartz and Holzman questioned them about what worked and what didn't, they raised issues that needed addressing before a second reading a month later. This reading took place before studio executives at Universal, including the head of Universal Studios, Stacey Snider. The reading went well enough that Universal management agreed to fund the remaining five readings to polish the show.

At this point, a new partner entered. David Stone was a Broadway producer who had met Platt while producing *The Diary of Anne Frank* on Broadway. While *Wicked* was still being developed, Platt had invited Stone to join him in producing the play once they were ready for a complete reading. Stone flew from New York to Los Angeles for the reading there. He was greatly affected by the show and threw himself into the job of producer. Working from the office of his production company in Manhattan, he created a budget and started consideration of the preproduction tasks of lining up a director, a choreographer, and designers for the show.

Schwartz and Holzman proceeded to hold two more readings at Universal and two more workshop readings at rehearsal studios in New York City. Finally, in March 2001, they did a complete reading of the play with the score and songs. The response of the audience was overwhelmingly positive. It was time to move to the next level of production.

Moving Forward

The play had now been developed to a point where Platt felt they could start planning for a Broadway start date. He wanted to be ready by 2003. To accomplish this, he had to find a director who could guide the play through the final readings and preproduction phase for the Broadway opening. Platt felt the director had to be an established professional familiar with all the aspects of putting on a Broadway musical—production, administration, and marketing—under the high-pressure Broadway conditions. That's not how things turned out. Stone felt it was more important to have a director with the right vision and the ability to handle a Broadway performance than one who had already worked on Broadway musicals. Several of the shows that Stone had produced on Broadway had been directed by Joe Mantello. Stone believed that Mantello had the ability to direct a musical—even though the only musical directing experience he had was doing *Dead Man Walking* for the San Francisco Opera Company. One of the points he made to the rest of the creative team was that Mantello had directed a variety of new plays, so he knew how to work with writers to hone their shows. When Mantello read the script he was enthusiastic—and he identified elements that worked in the play as well as issues that needed to be addressed. Schwartz was familiar with Mantello's work, and because of the bold way Mantello had staged nonmusical plays, Schwartz agreed to hire him as director for *Wicked*. Gregory Maguire, who had the right of approval, also agreed.

One of Mantello's first actions was to replace Stephanie Block as Elphaba. The show revolved around the character of Elphaba, and Mantello felt that having an actress experienced in Broadway musicals was important, especially given his own inexperience in the genre. To get the role of Elphaba cast as quickly as possible, Mantello scheduled auditions for the role for September 2001. Idina Menzel, who had played Maureen in *Rent*, among other roles, was acting in a musical version of Giuseppe Verdi's opera *Aida* when she heard about the auditions. She says she found the story intriguing, but, according to Stephen Schwartz's biography, *Defying Gravity*, what really sold her on auditioning was the creative team. " … it was going to be directed by Joe Mantello and have music by Stephen Schwartz, and I didn't care if it was the phone book … I put on green lipstick and smoky black eye shadow and went to audition for the green girl." Schwartz was torn between Menzel and one other actress, but he decided that the chemistry between Kristin Chenoweth and Idina Menzel would be most effective. Menzel became Elphaba and started preparing for the first New York reading, which was scheduled for December 2001.

The reading was preceded by a two-week workshop in which the major characters who had been cast were supplemented by friends of Stephen Schwartz in the other roles, directed by Mantello. The actors had scripts in loose-leaf notebooks, allowing pages to be replaced as changes were made. After two weeks, it was time for the reading, and Gregory Maguire came to New York to attend it. Schwartz was extremely nervous about how he would respond to the musical, which varied significantly from his book. Seventy-five people formed the audience for the reading, including friends, industry professionals, and cast members' families. Stephen Oremus, who had been appointed musical director and arranger for the show, had taken over piano-playing duties for the reading. Schwartz, relieved of his accompanist responsibilities, positioned

Joe Mantello directed *Wicked* on Broadway.

himself where he could observe the audience and note their reactions—especially those of Gregory Maguire. The team had given Maguire the latest copy of the script, and Schwartz was extremely nervous about how he would respond to the significant changes they had made to his work. However, Maguire was as engaged as the rest of the audience, and when the performance ended, he rose and applauded, leading the audience in a standing ovation. He didn't think the show was perfect, but he was impressed. Schwartz needn't have worried about Maguire's response to the musical's differences from the story in the novel. Maguire's attitude was: I changed *The*

Wonderful Wizard of Oz when I wrote my book; they have the right to change my story when they write their play.

The next reading was held back in Los Angeles, and it had to impress people as important to the project, in their own way, as Gregory Maguire—the senior executives of Universal Pictures, who had to approve funding for the full mounting of the play. Luckily for everyone, the reading in Los Angeles was successful, and Universal Pictures agreed to provide a significant part of the fourteen million dollars that would be required for the Broadway production. The rest of the money was raised by Platt and Stone in their role as producers. The budget called for four million of the fourteen million to be spent on sets.

The End and the Beginning

Now that the team had their funding, the pace of preparations intensified with an endless round of rehearsals and the hiring of actors and production crew members. One of the issues that remained unresolved was how to end the play. Initially, Schwartz and Holzman had planned to end it with Elphaba in the Badlands outside of Oz, devoting herself to healing the animals affected by the Wizard's actions. The fact that this would show Elphaba doing something good that no one will ever know about was important to Schwartz, who had wanted to ask the question of whether people can seem to us to be irredeemable monsters, when the truth is more complex. Mantello wanted a different ending, however. He felt that there were issues that needed to be cleared up by the ending.

On April 3, 2003, these activities culminated in the first out-of-town tryout at the Curran Theatre in San Francisco. It's usual for plays destined for Broadway to first be performed out of town, in other cities. Sometimes the out-of-town response to a play is so poor that it closes without ever getting to New York City. In other cases, shows are saved when flaws are identified and corrected, allowing the show to open successfully on Broadway. Schwartz insisted that they needed a three-month break between the completion of the tryouts and the play's Broadway opening. Schwartz was adamant about this because if major changes were needed, it wouldn't be possible to make them while in the middle of the San Francisco performances or while setting up in New York. The producers were reluctant but finally agreed. Doing so cost them one million dollars because they had to pay everyone while they were on break. This break would provide Schwartz and Holzman time to do any rewriting without having to make changes while the play was running on Broadway. Among the elements that were changed as a result of the San Francisco tryout was making Elphaba more appealing and less serious by giving her a sense of humor.

Designing Oz

In order to find the right scene designer for *Wicked*, Mantello came up with the idea of holding design auditions, which were held in Stone's office. Designers' approaches varied. Some verbally described their concept; others came with computer-generated renderings. Designer Eugene

Designer Eugene Lee's stunning set featured the Clock of the Time Dragon.

Lee, who had worked on shows such as *Sweeney Todd*, showed up with something more than a computer-generated image—he brought a model complete with Victorian-themed gadgets. It was exactly the opposite of what Mantello had envisioned as the setting for the play. Although Mantello had expected to use sleek modern high-tech sets, he immediately saw how Lee's version could work for the show, and Lee was hired. Lee, along with associate designer Edward Pierce and assistant designer Nick Francone, set out to design Oz. It was no small undertaking, since the script called for twenty scene changes. This meant that they would have to design an environment that could serve for various locations, rather than designing different sets for each scene. Set pieces would be flown in and out, and furniture moved on and off to different locations as the show progressed.

Maguire's novel features the Clock of the Time Dragon, which is a complicated wagon-drawn clockwork building topped by a dragonhead. Rather than telling time, the "clock" shows people secrets from their lives. For Maguire, it represented both the artificiality of the Wizard's rule and at the same time the concept that a girl born inside it (Elphaba) might be immune to such spectacle and wizardry. Lee made the Clock of the Time Dragon the centerpiece for his set.

Marc Platt was quite taken with the bold yet whimsical costume designs presented by designer Susan Hilferty at the design auditions, and she was hired. The final design for *Wicked's* Oz combined elements of the William Denslow illustrations from the original 1900 edition of *The*

Production wardrobe supervisor Alyce Gilbert shows one of the *Wicked* costumes.

Wonderful Wizard of Oz with the original elements inspired by the tone of Schwartz and Holzman's script. Wayne Cilento, the choreographer of the rock musical *Tommy*, was hired to do the choreography for the show. William Brohn was brought onboard to score the show for a full orchestra.

Now that the designers were in place, all that remained was to complete casting. British actress Shelley Carole was chosen to play Madame Morrible. Norbert Leo Butz became Fiyero, and Michelle Federer was given the role of Nessarose. In addition, singers and dancers had to be hired for the ensemble. As hundreds of costumes were produced and fitted, and contractors built the set, the producers, Stone and Platt, turned their attention to the show's public image. Working with the advertising agency Serino Coyne, Inc., they came up with the show's striking poster, which features a black and a white witch on a green background. The drawing is sleek and simple but designed to give the effect of opposites coming together. Finally, rehearsals for the San Francisco debut were held, and the final road-to-Broadway phase began.

Chapter 3

Reaching the Great White Way

Although the script was inspired by Maguire's novel, when it was finalized, the story in the musical version of *Wicked* differed significantly from the story in the book.

The Story

Act I starts with the population of Oz celebrating the fact that the Wicked Witch of the West, Elphaba, is dead. Glinda appears, and a citizen asks if she and Elphaba were friends. She proceeds to tell them the story of her and Elphaba's relationship.

The story shifts to the past. Glinda (then named Galinda) is studying at Shiz University when Elphaba and her sister arrive there. Although Elphaba is technically the

Opposite: Creative lighting helps project the sense of Elphaba's power.

The striking poster for *Wicked* captures the contrast between Glinda and Elphaba.

daughter of the governor of Munchkinland, it is implied that her real father was a mysterious visitor to her parents' home, a man who brought with him a bottle of green elixir, which Elphaba's mother tasted. Because Elphaba was born with green skin, her father loathed her and favored her wheelchair-bound, younger sister, Nessarose. The sisters arrive together at the university, and when he leaves, their father gives Nessarose a pair of silver slippers. The headmistress, Madame Morrible, takes charge of Nessarose, and Elphaba finds herself rooming with the pretty and popular, but shallow, Galinda. In her frustration at being separated from Nessarose, Elphaba inadvertently causes a spontaneous explosion. Madame Morrible, realizing that Elphaba has magical power, decides to teach her sorcery. Further, she tells Elphaba that because of her powers, she might be able to work with the Wonderful Wizard of Oz, something Elphaba has always wanted to do.

Galinda resents Elphaba because Madame Morrible will teach magic only to Elphaba, not to her. At the same time, Elphaba resents Galinda because of her popularity. They are constantly at odds. They take a history class with Dr. Dillamond, the sole Animal professor at the university. Dr. Dillamond is starting to experience the discrimination against sentient Animals that is spreading through Oz, even among the students. Dr. Dillamond explains to Elphaba that there is a conspiracy afoot to stop Animals from speaking. Elphaba wants to inform the Wizard, who she believes will stop it.

A young prince, Fiyero, arrives at Shiz, and Galinda is charmed by him. The students plan a party for that evening. When Galinda offers Elphaba a hat to wear to the party, Elphaba begins to think that maybe Galinda isn't so bad after all, but the hat is a witch's hat, meant to make Elphaba look ridiculous. Not realizing that Galinda intended to humiliate her, Elphaba asks Madame Morrible to let Galinda join the sorcery class, and Madame Morrible agrees.

Elphaba arrives at the party wearing the witch's hat, and the other students laugh at her. She dances alone. But when Madame Morrible tells Galinda that Elphaba asked her to let Galinda join her class, Galinda feels guilty about her treatment of Elphaba. She dances with Elphaba, and eventually everyone else joins them. The two are now friends, and back in their room they exchange confidences. Galinda tells Elphaba she intends to marry Fiyero, and Elphaba reveals that her father blames her for the death of

Elphaba and Glinda confront each other during a *Wicked* production number.

her mother in childbirth with Nessarose because of the steps she took to ensure that Nessarose didn't turn out green like Elphaba. Galinda decides to help Elphaba become popular.

Dr. Dillamond tells the students that he is leaving because Animals are no longer allowed to teach. Elphaba wants to protest this, but no one will join her. The students are shown a new technological tool—a cage whose purpose is to control Animals so they don't learn to speak. Elphaba is outraged, and she and Fiyero grab the cage, which holds a lion cub, and run off. The cub, it is implied, will grow up to be the Cowardly Lion.

Elphaba begins to fall for Fiyero, who has to leave to set the lion cub free. Madame Morrible tells Elphaba that the Wizard wants to meet her. Galinda tries to win Fiyero's respect by changing her name to "Glinda," which is how Dr. Dillamond always pronounced it, but Fiyero is wrapped up in saying goodbye to Elphaba. Elphaba invites Glinda to go to the Emerald City with her to meet the Wizard, and when the girls meet with him, Elphaba asks him to stop the suppression of the Animals. He says he will grant her request if she proves herself. Madame Morrible appears; she is now the Wizard's press secretary, and she presents Elphaba with a grimmerie—an ancient book of spells. Only those who are gifted magically can read it. When, at the Wizard's request, Elphaba tries a levitation spell from the book on one of the Wizard's monkey servants, it grows wings instead of rising. She realizes that the Wizard is suppressing the Animals and that she's been tricked into performing a spell that affects all of the Wizard's monkey servants, not just one. Further, she recognizes that the Wizard has no magical powers and could not read the grimmerie himself. The Wizard offers the girls everything they've ever dreamed of if they will assist him, but Elphaba runs away. In order to prevent Elphaba from revealing the truth that the Wizard is a powerless charlatan, Madame Morrible spreads the word that Elphaba is "wicked" and is behind the Animal trouble. Elphaba realizes that she must not let anyone hold her down, that she must do what's best for herself. She performs the play's signature song, "Defying Gravity," and flies.

Act II opens after some time has passed. Elphaba is now known as the Wicked Witch of the West because of her opposition to the Wizard, whereas Glinda has become Glinda the Good, for her public support of the Wizard's administration. Fiyero has accepted an appointment as captain of the guard for the Wizard, in an attempt to find Elphaba. Without his consent, Madame Morrible announces Fiyero's engagement to Glinda. Nessarose has become the governor of Munchkinland and has been oppressing the Munchkins. Elphaba casts a spell to make Nessarose able to walk by turning her silver slippers into ruby ones, but as a result, Nessarose's Munchkin lover, Boq, decides she doesn't need him anymore. Nessarose casts a spell on him from Elphaba's grimmerie, but the spell goes awry, and Elphaba has to save Boq—by making him into a tin man.

Elphaba goes back to the Wizard's palace, intending to free the monkey servants. She encounters the Wizard, who offers to redeem her reputation if she'll work with him. However, upon meeting Dr. Dillamond, who can no longer speak, she swears to keep opposing the Wizard. Fiyero helps Elphaba escape and accompanies her. Elphaba and Fiyero swear they will always be together.

Glinda suggests to the Wizard and Madame Morrible that they trap Elphaba by making her believe Nessarose is in trouble. Elphaba suddenly has a vision of the flying house that crushes Nessarose. Outside Dorothy's house, Glinda and Elphaba argue over Fiyero, and when guards arrive to capture Elphaba, she realizes that Glinda is responsible for the flying house that has killed her sister. Fiyero holds Glinda hostage so that Elphaba can get away, but he is captured by the guards. Recognizing that Fiyero loves Elphaba, Glinda tells them not to hurt him, but they ignore her, taking him to a field for interrogation. Elphaba attempts to protect him with a spell, and he winds up as the Scarecrow.

Elphaba vows to live up to her reputation as the Wicked Witch of the West, and she captures Dorothy, refusing to release her until she gives her Nessarose's slippers. Madam Morrible, assisted by Boq, convinces the people of Oz to assist in rescuing Dorothy. Glinda attempts to warn Elphaba, but Elphaba refuses to free Dorothy. Elphaba and Glinda forgive each other for their actions, and Elphaba gives the grimmerie to Glinda. They say goodbye forever, acknowledging the influence they have had on each other. A mob reaches the castle where Elphaba is residing. Glinda watches from the shadows as Dorothy throws a bucket of water on Elphaba, who melts. Grief-stricken, Glinda takes Elphaba's black hat and the small bottle of green elixir.

Back at the Emerald City, Glinda confronts the Wizard with Elphaba's bottle. When he realizes that he was Elphaba's real father, the Wizard breaks down in remorse. Glinda banishes him from Oz and has Madame Morrible imprisoned for murdering Nessarose.

Fiyero, in scarecrow form, goes to the castle where Elphaba was hiding. At the place where she melted, he knocks on the floor, and Elphaba appears from a trap door, revealing that the whole episode was a ploy. Now that her enemies think she is dead, she is free to spend her future with Fiyero, although she is sorry she'll never see Glinda again. Returning to the musical's beginning, Glinda tells the citizens of Oz that the Wicked Witch of the West is dead and swears she'll earn her title as Glinda the Good. While the people of Oz celebrate, Glinda mourns, and Elphaba and Fiyero leave Oz.

The Curran Theatre in San Francisco, where *Wicked* had its out-of-town tryout

San Francisco Tryout

Now that the play was going public, there was a final review of the script by Universal's lawyers, who wanted to make sure that it didn't infringe on MGM's rights by mimicking anything in the movie. For example, to avoid having Glinda's entrance look too much like that of her namesake in the MGM movie, she arrives in a gray metal ring, surrounded by myriad small bubbles from a bubble-blowing machine, instead of showing up inside one big bubble. One proposed change that incensed Schwartz was the demand that all lines referring to events in the movie be cut. He felt this damaged the concept of the script as a prequel to the events in the film, and it cut some of the show's biggest laughs, which resulted from sly references to the film. Schwartz lost many battles over the changes to the script, but he won that one. The lawyers didn't want Nessarose's shoes to turn to ruby slippers. Schwartz wanted them to turn from silver (as in the book) to red. After a long dispute, he finally got agreement that the slippers could be lit by a red spotlight so that they appeared to turn red.

One of the play's two acts was given a dress rehearsal two days prior to the first performance, and the other was given a dress rehearsal one day before. Thus, the first time the play was performed in its entirety was the opening night of the San Francisco tryout. With Schwartz, watching from the back of the theater, obsessing about how dark the opening scene seemed, the sixteen hundred people in the audience watched the play. When it was over, the audience leapt to their feet in a standing ovation. Schwartz, at last, relaxed—but not for long. He had been taking notes during the show and showed up at a breakfast meeting with Mantello, Stone, Platt, and Holzman the next morning with a long list of things that he felt needed to be changed. This antagonized the director, who already felt that Schwartz didn't trust him to do his job. The fact is, the show worked pretty well—it just didn't match the vision Schwartz had in his head. His list included a significant

FACTS ABOUT *WICKED*

Broadway Run:
October 30, 2003–present

Venue: Gershwin Theatre

Number of Performances: 5,819 as of October 8, 2017

Gross Revenues: $1.1 billion as of August 2017

Original Cast
Glinda: Kristin Chenoweth
Elphaba: Idina Menzel
Fiyero: Norbert Leo Butz
Nessarose: Michelle Federer
Boq: Christopher Fitzgerald
The Wonderful Wizard of Oz: Joel Grey
Madame Morrible: Carole Shelley
Doctor Dillamond: William Youmans

Popular Songs
No One Mourns the Wicked — Glinda and Citizens of Oz
The Wizard and I — Madame Morrible and Elphaba
Popular — Glinda
I'm Not That Girl — Elphaba
Defying Gravity — Elphaba, Glinda, Guards, and Citizens of Oz
As Long As You're Mine — Elphaba and Fiyero
For Good — Glinda and Elphaba

Awards

2004 New York Drama Desk Awards

Outstanding New Musical

Outstanding Book of a Musical — Winnie Holzman

Outstanding Director of a Musical — Joe Mantello

Outstanding Lyrics — Stephen Schwartz

Outstanding Set Design of a Musical — Eugene Lee

Outstanding Costume Design — Susan Hilferty

2004 Tony Awards

Best Actress in a Musical — Idina Menzel

Best Scenic Design — Eugene Lee

Best Costume Design — Susan Hilferty

2005 Grammy Awards

Best Cast Album

amount of material that he felt should be cut because the show ran too long—the performance had taken three hours and twenty minutes. Major cuts meant that actors would have to perform scenes differently, and the orchestra would have to learn new versions of the score—and there was only one week before the Broadway opening. In the Stephen Schwartz biography, *Defying Gravity*, Schwartz recounts an incident that changed his attitude. As he left the hotel where the meeting had taken place, he saw an enormous crowd standing in front of the nearby theater where the play was being performed. Given his propensity to worry, he thought there must have been an accident—until he realized that he was looking at an enormous line of people extending from the theater's box office. Word-of-mouth raves from the first-night audience had created an enormous demand for tickets.

Costuming the Citizens of Oz

Much of how an audience perceives a play's characters depends on the clothes they wear. Costume designer Susan Hilferty was charged with creating the "look" for the denizens of Oz. Because of the fantastical nature of Oz, she had to create clothing for an alternative universe, but it had to be recognizable and reflect the nature of the characters in a way the audience could relate to. To accomplish this task, she researched the period from 1900 to 1920, when L. Frank Baum wrote the Oz books. The result was a style Hilferty refers to as "twisted Edwardian." In her designs, basic outfits that would have been worn around 1900 are altered to be off-center, asymmetrical, or warped in some

Susan Hilferty used stylized historical costumes to emphasize the nature of the characters.

way. She also used costume design to emphasize the themes of the play. For example, in the Shiz University scene, she combined recognizable elements of a school uniform with bizarre design, representing the characters' struggle between conformity and individuality. Likewise, in the Emerald City scene, she incorporated fur and feathers into the costumes, to emphasize the upper-class citizens' indifference to the fate of the Animals.

From the Emerald City to Broadway

The time finally came to move the show to Broadway. The gigantic set had to be transported all the way across the

LIGHT AND SOUND

Everything about *Wicked* is complex, from the script with its subplots to the intricate clockwork set. The sound and light requirements for the show are no exception. Because there is a single major set that is altered in each scene, rather than different sets for different scenes, the lighting must define each location in the story. Lighting designer Kenneth Posner employed eight hundred theatrical lights, some of which were computer-controlled, to allow him to reposition them during the show. Because light alters the skin tone of actors onstage, the lighting must also be adjusted to make the cast's skin color appear natural. In *Wicked: The Grimmerie, A Behind-the-Scenes Look at the Hit Broadway Musical*, Posner says, "I built a career not making people look green onstage." In this sense, *Wicked* was a departure for him. Whenever Elphaba is onstage, she has to be lit with a green light to maximize her green coloring. Posner worked with makeup artist Joe Dulude to find the right shade of light for the character, and he had to establish a lighting scheme for each of the show's fifty-four scenes to maintain the proper mood. His most challenging scene was the Emerald City because he had to create lighting that accommodated the green scenery, the green costumes, and the largest song-and-dance number in the show.

The sound designer, Tony Meola, had two tasks—design the sound and sound effects for the show, and create the sound system for the theater. His job was to make sure that everyone in the audience could hear the orchestra, the singers, and the dialogue without having any one element drown another out—no easy task. When placing speakers, he had to work around the giant clock mechanism that occupied the center of the stage. Meola prides himself on giving the impression that the sound the audience hears is coming from the stage, not from visible stacks of speakers, so he hid speakers on either side of the Dragon Clock as well as in the vines at the sides of the stage. He was also responsible for the show's sound effects—and it had quite a few. Meola created many of them using wood available from the construction of the giant set. In a 2003 interview, he said, "I wanted to create a mechanical sound to all the effects, using a cacophony of creaking and groaning wood-based sounds to create an eerie impression of the various animals, other strange creatures, the inside workings of the clock, etc." The show features a giant mechanical Wizard's head, whose facial features move, operated by an actor backstage. Meola created a variety of clinking and clanking sounds to accompany the raising and lowering of its eyebrows, the opening and closing of its mouth, and the swiveling of its head.

country, from San Francisco to New York City, by truck. The Gershwin Theatre is cavernous. According to Winnie Holzman, in a 2004 *Playbill* interview, "It's a barn. Stephen and I walked in there before they loaded the set, and we were just staring at it. We looked at each other with terror in our eyes. We were intimidated. But [set designer] Eugene Lee knew exactly what to do. Once the set was in, we never felt that same fear." The set couldn't be installed, however, until Holzman, Schwartz, and Mantello agreed that they had the final version of the play—otherwise, something in the set might needed to be altered. Even though the show had been a popular and financial success in San Francisco, the creative team felt it had to be stronger for Broadway. The three argued endlessly over changes in the script. Finally they arrived at a definitive version of the play, which required several of the roles to be recast, including the Wizard. Veteran Broadway star Joel Grey was brought in to play the role.

The designers weren't exempt from changes either. When the colorful costumes arrived for the big University of Shiz party dance scene, Mantello thought they took the focus off the principal actors, and he asked Susan Hilferty to remake the outfits for the entire production number in black and white. Every scene in which Elphaba appeared had changes. Schwartz and Holzman cut a scene of Dr. Dillamond's funeral, which they felt was unnecessary, especially since Dillamond wasn't actually dead. Even that caused contention. Mantello pointed out that it was the first scene in which Elphaba wears black, which explains why she always wears black for the rest of the show. Schwartz

The Gershwin Theatre, where *Wicked* premiered in New York City

IT'S NOT EASY BEING GREEN

Being a Wicked Witch isn't easy. It took Idina Menzel about forty minutes to paint herself green before each show.

argued that the scene needed to go, and that the audience wouldn't care why Elphaba dressed in black. There was also a huge disagreement between Mantello and Schwartz as to the appropriate song and staging for the party scene at Shiz University. Schwartz was, in fact, still extremely nervous over the success of the show he'd worked so hard to create.

On October 7, 2003, *Wicked* opened with its first preview, in preparation for opening night, October 30. The show had been cut to two hours and forty-five minutes from over three hours. Schwartz felt that the longer version was more moving, but there was no question it ran too long and had to be trimmed. The preview audience, however, loved the new version. Schwartz was still panicking, and his response to panic was to issue ultimatums: make this change, or I'll quit the show. By now, producer David Stone had learned to simply let these tantrums pass, waiting until Schwartz took back his resignation. A week before opening night, the show was frozen, which meant that no further changes could be made. This allowed the company time to polish the final version before the critics saw it.

When the show opened on October 30, 2003, the reviews from the critics were mixed, and many were outright negative. *New York Times* reviewer Ben Brantley clearly considered the show heavy-handed in its parallels to the contemporary American political scene. "Lightness of touch is not the salient characteristic of this politically indignant deconstruction of L. Frank Baum's 'Oz' tales," he wrote, although he felt that Kristin Chenoweth sparkled in her role as Glinda. Charles Isherwood's review in *Variety* was even more critical: "A strenuous effort to be all things to all people tends to weigh down this lumbering, overstuffed $14 million production. 'Wicked' is stridently earnest one minute, self-mocking the next; a fantastical allegory about the perils of fascism in one scene, a Nickelodeon special about the importance of inner beauty in another … but the musical itself truly soars only on rare occasions, usually when one of its two marvelously talented leading ladies, Kristin Chenoweth and Idina Menzel, unleashes the kind of vocal magic that needs no supernatural or even technical assistance." In general, the notices for the stars, Kristin Chenoweth and Idina Menzel, were rapturous. The two performers unquestionably played a major role in the show's success.

In contrast to the unflattering reviews, the word-of-mouth reports from people who had seen it were overwhelmingly positive. This dichotomy is evident in the ratings *Wicked* received on the Broadway World website, where its average score from the critics was only 5.33 out of 10, but its score from audiences was 9.2 out 10. It was a "feel-good" show, and the public embraced it. *Wicked* was nominated for Best Score, Best Musical, and Best Book at the 2004 Tony Awards, but lost out to *Avenue Q*. Idina Menzel won for Best Actress.

Idina Menzel received the 2004 Tony Award for Best Actress for playing Elphaba.

In defiance of the critics, *Wicked* has run for more than thirteen years and is still going. There are a number of possible reasons for this. First, there is the appeal of *The Wizard of Oz* itself—that is, the MGM movie. In a Dramatist's Guild interview presented on YouTube, Stephen Schwartz says that one important fact the team realized during the readings was that they couldn't do anything that contradicted the film version. For most people, the movie represented the reality of Oz, and while audiences were delighted to see more of the characters' stories, these had to conform to the "reality" of the film. The universal appeal of the film and the popularity of Maguire's book (and its three sequels) create a natural audience for the play. Schwartz's cleverness in giving the story an upbeat ending leaves the audience feeling good and more likely to recommend the play to others. Reviewers may feel that downbeat endings are more meaningful, but ordinary people like to leave the theater happy. A similar point can be made about the production values of the play. Whereas many critics considered the special effects overblown, the costumes garish, and the production numbers overelaborate, Broadway audiences like spectacle. The choice of the creative team to make the show larger than life was apparently the right one. Above all, there was the relationship between the two leads, played impeccably by the spunky Kristin Chenoweth and the dramatic Idina Menzel. It is not accidental that the actresses who later replaced them tried to capture the tone of the two leads' original performances. Years after its opening, *Wicked* is still drawing sell-out audiences. Making a return visit to the show after ten years, critic Charles Isherwood had this to say, "A return visit reveals that the producers have been careful, not to say monomaniacal, about replicating the experience they gave audiences in the opening months. Remarkably, they continue to secure performers who can both fill the (hefty) vocal and (less taxing) acting demands of the central roles, the "good" witch Glinda and the "wicked" one, Elphaba, as well as evoke the distinctive styles of the stars who put their imprint on them."

Although the show is calculated to appeal to whole families, there's little doubt that its largest audience is teenage girls, many of whom identify with issues faced by the two girls in the play, the search for identity and the feeling of being an outcast. The story doesn't appeal just to teenage girls, however, but to women of all ages. Elysa Gardner of *USA Today* was a rare critic who loved the show: "It's too soon to tell whether Schwartz's score

The Wicked Witch of the West threatens Dorothy in the MGM 1939 movie *The Wizard of Oz.*

for *Wicked*, which opened Thursday at the Gershwin Theatre, will prove as enduring. But it's safe to say that this is the most complete, and completely satisfying, new musical I've come across in a long time." She also noted that Winnie Holzman "provides a libretto that juggles winning irreverence with thoughtfulness and heart." Many male reviewers have commented, in a derogatory manner, on the fact that the show attracts mostly girls and women, many of them implying that its success is due only to its appeal to teenage girls. What they seem to miss is that it is also a girlfriend play. There have been few plays that focus on female friendships and issues. Women are most often secondary characters, as in *Les Misérables*, or the love interest, as in *The Phantom of the Opera*. Author Charlaine Harris, in an article titled "The Musical 'Wicked' Is As Much About Feminism As It Is About Witches," wrote, "At its heart, *Wicked* is a tale of friendship, and how deep, platonic bonds can change a person 'For Good.'" Although there haven't been many plays that focus on women's relationships, there have been quite a number of movies, from *Clueless* to *Thelma and Louise*. Movies and plays that deal with relationships in general tend to appeal more to women than to men, and for shows that deal with relationships between women, this is even more true. The simple fact is that people tend to be most interested in those who are like themselves. Thus, saying that *Wicked* appeals primarily to women is like saying that a show about motorcycles appeals mainly to motorcyclists. Kevin Fallon, in a 2013 article titled, "A 'Wicked' Decade: How a Critically Trashed Musical Became a Long-Running Smash," sums it up: "It's about a friendship that blossoms between adversaries, at once a love story between these two girls and an underdog tale. Elphaba is the ugly ducking turned all-powerful swan, and anyone who's lived in the shadow of a Glinda can relate to that."

Chapter 4

Wicked Influence

Wicked has the distinction of having hit the $1 billion revenue mark faster than any other show on Broadway. It has had a national tour and has been mounted in cities around the world. Part of the show's success is due to the universal popularity of *The Wizard of Oz* itself and the success of Maguire's book. However, it also has an appeal of its own. *Wicked* provides great spectacle and a female-oriented coming-of-age story that explores the choices that people—in particular women—are forced to make, and the way society paints them in response to those choices. For many women, especially young women, the story of a young woman finding her power resonates strongly.

Opposite: Many young women relate to the idea of the popular girl vs. the outsider in *Wicked*.

Wicked's Influence

Wicked is not groundbreaking in the sense of bringing something new in the way of a production to Broadway. Rather, it is evolutionary. It is the natural outgrowth of the shows on Broadway that have been successful in the past. It harkens back to the heyday of musicals in the 1960s, when Rodgers and Hammerstein enjoyed enormous success with shows that featured emotional relationships and impressive production numbers. Since the 1990s, massive spectacular productions such as *The Phantom of the Opera* and *The Lion King* have wowed audiences, convincing the ticket-buying public that it's worth shelling out over $100 per ticket. Many New York critics complain that modern Broadway musicals consist more of showmanship than substance, but musicals have always reflected the times and music of the period in which they were written and produced. In the pre-1960s era, the songs from musical shows often became hits on the radio. One of the criticisms of *Wicked* is the way it is orchestrated. Reviewers feel that it is too loud and bombastic, but *Wicked* reflects present culture, in which rock and roll is the predominant popular

Facts You May Not Know

MOVING OZ

For the 2005 national tour, the sets, costumes, and props required fourteen 52-foot (16 meter) tractor-trailer trucks to transport them from city to city.

musical form—and loud, dramatic rock music, in turn, reflects our loud and dramatic present culture. *Wicked* and the grand musicals that have preceded it in the past twenty years give audiences what they want—entertainment.

Wicked speaks to an important change our culture has been going through in the late twentieth and early twenty-first centuries—women taking charge of their own lives. Critic Charles Isherwood returned to see the show in 2014, ten years after he originally reviewed it. In his 2014 *New York Times* review, Isherwood says, "In retrospect, 'Wicked' seems an early sign of the cultural clout—which is to say buying power—of a generation of girls (and now women) whose desire to see, and read, and sing along with stories about female empowerment has become a snowballing trend." In a *Time Out New York* interview, Idina Menzel was asked, "Who is Elphaba to you?" She responded, "Elphaba is a little bit of every girl/woman I know who is struggling to find themselves, to harness their power and to believe in their unconventional beauty." Stephen Schwartz's answer in a YouTube interview to the question of why *Wicked* continues to be popular is even simpler: "There is a green girl inside all of us."

According to Schwartz, *Wicked* wasn't aimed at teenagers. In an interview in *Ecumenica: Journal of Theatre and Performance*, he says, "It's about an outsider struggling with her 'outsider-ness,' if you will. I think these are themes and characters that speak to teenagers and what they are going through." In 2018, the stage version of Disney's musical film *Frozen* will be opening on Broadway. Given previous

Top Ten Longest-Running Musicals

According to *Playbill*, the following is the list of longest-running musicals on Broadway. The number after the title is the number of performances.

1. *The Phantom of the Opera*   12,254
2. *Chicago* (1996 Revival)   8,579
3. *The Lion King*   8,180
4. *Cats*   7,485
5. *Les Misérables*   6,680
6. *A Chorus Line*   6,137
7. *Oh! Calcutta!* (1976 Revival)   5,959
8. *Wicked*   *5,835*
9. *Mamma Mia!*   5,773
10. *Beauty and the Beast*   5,461

As of October 22, 2017, *Wicked* was the eighth longest-running show, but quickly heading toward becoming the seventh.

Top Ten Highest-Grossing Musicals

According to *Playbill*, the following is the list of highest-grossing Broadway musicals as of August, 2017. The number after the title is each play's gross revenue (not adjusted for inflation).

1. *The Lion King* $1,396, 638,949
2. *Wicked* $1,134,379,492
3. *Phantom of the Opera* $1,117,096,453
4. *Mamma Mia!* $624,391,693
5. *Chicago* (1996 revival) $593,302,223
6. *Jersey Boys* $558,416,084
7. *The Book of Mormon* $506,681,955
8. *Beauty and the Beast* $429,158,458
9. *Les Misérables* $406,528,901
10. *Cats* $342,207,841

Wicked is the second highest-grossing Broadway musical of all time.

Disney shows such as *The Lion King*, it too will no doubt be a lavish production. As in *Wicked*, its protagonists will be young women, royal sisters Elsa and Anna. Like Elphaba, Elsa doesn't fit neatly into her world. The show is likely to appeal to the same audiences as *Wicked*, and it is equally likely to face similar commentary on the part of critics.

Wicked in Popular Culture

Wicked has achieved the ultimate sign of modern success: inclusion in other media. This Broadway musical has played a role in the plot of episodes of various popular television programs, among them *Brothers & Sisters*, *The War at Home*, *New Girl*, and *Ugly Betty*. For filming purposes, the latter used the Pantages Theatre in Los Angeles to represent the Gershwin Theatre on Broadway, for an episode titled "Something Wicked This Way Comes." Most notably, the television series *Glee* used songs from *Wicked* as plot devices in four different episodes. In the "Wheels" episode, two students competed for a lead solo by singing the song "Defying Gravity;" in the "New York" episode, the same students sang a duet of "For Good" on the stage of the Gershwin Theatre; on the show's one-hundredth episode, three students sang "Defying Gravity" together; and in the series' second-to-last episode, those students sang "Popular." A clip of the song "Popular" was also used in the 2009 movie *Zombieland*.

The songs themselves have been used and altered by a variety of entertainers. Actor/singer John Barrowman, who played Jack on the *Dr. Who* and *Torchwood* TV series, adapted the lyrics of "The Wizard and I" to "The Doctor

"Defying Gravity," the show-stopping song by Elphaba at the end of Act I, is *Wicked*'s most famous song. Elphaba's powerful rendition, combined with the special effect of her rising into the air, creates an unmistakable impact as the first half of the play ends. When writing the song, Stephen Schwartz deliberately started it with simple notes, and then had it build as Elphaba's power manifests itself. Initially, Schwartz wrote the song as a solo for Elphaba. In its final version, there is a duet at the beginning and in the middle between Elphaba and Glinda. At one point in the show's development, Schwartz had written a bitter sarcastic song in which Glinda and Elphaba sing to each other, "I hope you're happy," as they accuse each other of making mistakes. The song "I Hope You're Happy" was cut from the show, but Schwartz incorporated one verse into "Defying Gravity." The two characters start by saying, "I hope you're happy" sarcastically, but end by saying the phrase sincerely. The song is sung at the point in the story when Elphaba is inviting Glinda to join her in fighting the Wizard. Glinda is tempted but can't bring herself to take the risk. This is when they part ways, and Elphaba becomes the Wicked Witch of the West. For that reason, Schwartz wanted the song to create a powerful impression, and he played to his strengths in writing it. In the biography *Defying Gravity*, he admits that he is at his best when writing songs that express anger, as in this song, which highlights Elphaba's defiance. Idina Menzel also had an influence on how the song was performed on the stage. When she first started working on the song with Schwartz, he had it pitched entirely in the alto range, but Menzel, who has a four-octave vocal range, suggested to him that as she rose into the sky, the notes of the song should rise into a higher range as well, and he adopted her idea.

and I" to sing on his 2008 UK tour. Three actresses who played Elphaba recorded their own versions of the song "Defying Gravity." Kerry Ellis, who played Elphaba in London's West End (London's equivalent of Broadway) and on Broadway in 2008, recorded her own rock version of "Defying Gravity," produced by British musician Brian May; the song is included on her 2010 album *Anthems* (2010). Louise Dearman, who played both Elphaba and Glinda in the West End, recorded an acoustic version of "Defying Gravity" for her *Here Comes the Sun* album. Rachel Tucker, who also played Elphaba in the West End, sang "Defying Gravity" on her *The Reason* album.

Wicked's songs and characters have been parodied in the anime series *Red Garden*, the daytime drama *Passions*, and the *Buffy the Vampire Slayer* graphic novels. Continuing the tradition of one show paying homage to another, the Broadway show *Shrek the Musical* parodies *Wicked's* Act I finale when the character Lord Farquaad mimics "Defying Gravity," proclaiming, "No one's gonna bring me down" atop his castle. Critics have noted that the song "Let It Go" from the Disney film *Frozen* has a theme and style similar to that of "Defying Gravity." This is not surprising since the original Elphaba, Idina Menzel, sang the song, which won an Oscar for best song.

Defying Stephen Schwartz

Gregory Maguire created an alternate version of L. Frank Baum's book, and Stephen Schwartz created an alternate version of Maguire's book—but the revisions don't end there. Ben Cohn, assistant conductor of the *Wicked* orchestra, has created an alternate version of Schwartz's songs in *Wicked*. In a project dubbed "Out of Oz," he has recorded studio versions of many of the songs in *Wicked* with different, simpler arrangements. In 2015, he released a YouTube video of the show's most famous song, "Defying Gravity," with a stripped-down, acoustic arrangement using piano and guitar, presenting the song as a duet between Rachel Tucker, who was playing Elphaba at the time, and Aaron Tveit, a former Fiyero. The live performance was shot in a studio in Brooklyn, New York. The video was viewed three million times in 2015 alone.

Cohn observed, "The songs are "really universal, and people listen to them on their own outside of the show, and we thought it could be cool to sort of give them a new life." Cohn's goal was to create a more intimate version of the songs. In the show, Elphaba is shouting the songs for all the world to hear, according to Cohn. He wanted to create a version that would be more personal.

Cohn has been with *Wicked* for years and said that he always wanted to re-envision the Schwartz tunes, strip them down, and take them out of context. For this project, Schwartz gave him free rein to create his own versions the songs. "Defying Gravity" was just the first in the "Out of Oz" project. Cohn has recorded other songs since that time, which are also available on YouTube.

When asked how Stephen Schwartz responded to the reworking of his material, Cohn said Schwartz blessed his attempt to make an alternate version of his songs, telling him to "go for it." Cohn said, "I think he was pleased with what he heard."

And the Story Goes On

There is no question that Gregory Maguire's book *Wicked* was popular before the musical hit Broadway. However, you can't have a show seen by tens of million of people without increasing the number of people who want to read the book. Ever since the publication of the original novel and the premiere of the play, fans have been demanding to know more of the backstories of the characters in *The Wizard of Oz*. In response, Maguire has written three sequels to Wicked:

- *Son of a Witch* (2005): This is the story of Elphaba's son, the hapless but determined Liir. The tale follows Liir on a dark journey through Maguire's alternate Land of Oz and into the Emerald City, which has been abandoned by the Wizard, where Liir falls into the clutches of dragons.

- *A Lion Among Men* (2008): The story overlaps with *Wicked* and *Son of a Witch* and carries the plot forward eight years beyond the second book. The book tells the story of the Cowardly Lion, Brrr—once the tiny cub protected by Elphaba. With Oz on the verge of civil war, Brrr approaches oracle Yackle in search of information about the Wicked Witch of the West. On his journey, he encounters a swamp of ghosts, trolls, and a forbidding cat princess as armies amass in Oz.

- *Out of Oz* (2011): Oz is racked with social unrest, Glinda is placed under house arrest, and the Cowardly

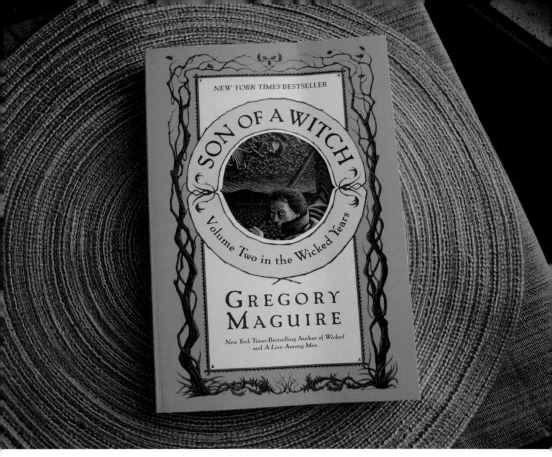

Gregory Maguire went on to write three sequels to his novel *Wicked*.

Lion is hiding from the law. Meanwhile, the Emerald City prepares to launch a war against Munchkinland. Dorothy returns to Oz, and the book ties up all loose ends from the series. *Out of Oz* is supposedly the last book in the series.

Wicked the Movie

Remember the movie version of *Wicked* that Marc Platt was working on at Universal when Stephen Schwartz entered his life? Well, it's back, albeit in a different form. Ever since

Wicked became a smash hit on Broadway, there have been discussions about a movie version of the musical. For many years, the creative team behind *Wicked* was reluctant to release a *Wicked* film, for fear of cutting into ticket sales for the musical. Instead, they decided to wait until a decrease in ticket sales indicated that the run was winding down. That decrease has yet to materialize. So, in April 2017, the project was finally given a release date: December 20, 2019.

In 2012, Universal Pictures confirmed that they'd obtained the film rights to the show. The movie is being produced by Platt's production company, Platt Productions, and Universal. To direct the production, they've chosen Stephen Daldry, who has experience in both film and Broadway directing. Winnie Holzman will write the screenplay, and it will of course feature Stephen Schwartz's music. Marc Platt and David Stone will produce the film, and Wayne Cilento will do the choreography. Cilento is an established choreographer who, in addition to *Wicked*, has choreographed such famous Broadway shows as *Sweet Charity*, *The Who's Tommy*, and *How to Succeed in Business Without Really Trying*.

One question facing the producers is who will play the leads in the film. Idina Menzel and Kristin Chenoweth created the roles of Elphaba and Glinda and have been the model for the actresses that followed them. However, they were thirty-one and thirty-five, respectively, when they started playing those roles on Broadway, and at this point, they are too old to pass for college-aged girls on the big screen. While it's possible for thirty-year-olds to pass as teenagers on a stage distant from the audience, it's much harder in a movie, where the audience views the actors close up.

According to UK tabloid the *Sun*, one singer under consideration to play Elphaba is former Pussycat Dolls singer Nicole Scherzinger. Scherzinger is interested in pursuing an acting career and has had early discussions with the film's producers. She has Broadway experience, having starred as Grizabella in *Cats* in 2015. She also performed the voice of Sina in Disney's *Moana* in 2016. Her choice would present a couple of issues, however. First, she doesn't have a great deal of acting experience, and a film as widely anticipated as this places a great deal of responsibility on the lead actress. And again, there's the issue of age. Scherzinger was thirty-eight in 2017, which means she'd be forty by the time the film was completed, and the producers have to consider whether she can pass for a college student. Other singers who have been considered in the past for the role, such as Lea Michele, Anna Kendrick, and Samantha Barks, face a similar problem. Perhaps the best solution would be to find a young rising star, as was the case with Idina Menzel when she premiered the role of Elphaba on Broadway.

Lasting Recognition

When Stephen Schwartz was growing up, seeing the names of great composers in the Theater Hall of Fame on the wall of the Gershwin Theatre inspired him to pursue a career as a Broadway composer. He wanted to see his name on that wall. In 2010, Stephen Schwartz finally achieved his lifelong ambition and was inducted into the Theater Hall of

Fame as a composer, having his name added in gold to the others around the walls of the Gershwin Theatre, including such greats as Irving Berlin and Stephen Sondheim. He was inducted by the producers of *Wicked*, Marc Platt and David Stone. In addition to the *Wicked* movie, Schwartz has embarked on a new project—turning the film *The Prince of Egypt*, for which he wrote the songs, into a stage musical.

After fourteen years, *Wicked* is still playing on Broadway to sold-out crowds. More than fifty million people have seen the show worldwide. In *Wicked: The Grimmerie, A Behind the Scenes Look at the Hit Broadway Musical*, Gregory Maguire is quoted as saying, "Basically, I have permanent gooseflesh now. It's a medical condition of having a play on Broadway. However many times I see the musical, I can hardly believe that there are so many people screaming and cheering for the Wicked Witch of the West."

Glossary

ACOUSTIC A type of music that uses non-electronic instruments.

ALTO The lowest range of the female voice.

ANIME A style of Japanese animation used in media and print works.

BOMBASTIC Inflated, overblown.

BOOK In musical theater, the non-music part of the show.

DEFINITIVE Defining or authoritative.

DENIZENS Inhabitants.

EDWARDIAN The period during which King Edward VII ruled England, from 1901 to 1910.

FLOWN In relation to backdrops or pieces of stage set, to lower from above by means of cables.

FROZEN The point in developing a show when no further changes are allowed.

GENRE Subcategory.

HAPLESS Unlucky.

ICONIC Representative of a particular concept.

IMPECCABLE Flawless.

INFRINGE To violate the rights of an entity.

LEITMOTIF A musical theme used for a particular character.

MYRIAD Many, numerous.

PARODY A creative work that makes fun of another work.

PROTAGONISTS The main characters.

RAPTUROUS Full of joy or delight.

REVISIONIST Restating a past work from a different point of view.

SARCASTIC Saying something but meaning the opposite, often to be insulting or funny.

SENTIENT Having self-awareness.

STORYBOARDING A technique in which each scene or major moment in a play or film is represented on a card to create a visual outline of the work.

VOCAL RANGE The number of musical octaves or different musical notes a person can sing.

Further Information

BOOKS

Cote, David. *Wicked: The Grimmerie, A Behind-the-Scenes Look at the Hit Broadway Musical.* New York, NY: Hyperion, 2005.

de Giere, Carol. *Defying Gravity: The Creative Career of Stephen Schwartz, from* Godspell *to* Wicked. Milwaukee, WI: Applause Theatre and Cinema Books, 2008.

Laird, Paul R. *Wicked: A Musical Biography* Lanham, MD: Scarecrow Press, 2011.

Moerbeek, Kees and Attenberg, Jami. *Wicked The Musical: A Pop-Up Compendium of Splendiferous Delight and Thrillifying Intrigue.* New York: Melcher Media, 2009.

WEBSITES

Playbill: Think You Know Everything About *Wicked*? Think Again.

http://www.playbill.com/article/think-you-know-everything-about-wicked-think-again

Composer Stephen Schwartz shares stories on a variety of *Wicked* subjects, including its history and the upcoming movie.

The 18 wonder witches of *Wicked* on Broadway

https://www.timeout.com/newyork/theater/wicked-on-broadway-talking-to-the-15-wonderful-witches

This page features interviews with eighteen women who have played Elphaba on Broadway, providing insight into what it was like performing in the show.

Wicked History

http://www.musicalschwartz.com/wicked-history.htm

This website provides articles on a variety of aspects of the show, including its history, songs, costumes, and more.

Wicked the Musical

https://wickedthemusical.com/media/

The official website of the show, it includes a news section that provides the latest information on the production.

VIDEOS

Writing Wicked—Winnie Holzman, Stephen Schwartz, Hosted by Michael Kerker—Dramatists Guild.

https://www.youtube.com/watch?v=_vBYgfik4NU.

Winnie Holzman and Stephen Schwartz discuss their experiences during the process of writing *Wicked*.

#OutofOz: "Defying Gravity" WICKED Studio Sessions
https://www.youtube.com/watch?v=EFbuID1QG0Y

The first video in the series Out of Oz: Wicked Studio Sessions, in which the *Wicked* performers sing reimagined versions of *Wicked* songs.

Wicked: The Musical Documentary, Part I
https://www.youtube.com/watch?v=9ZVp2ZOGAhw.

This documentary covers all aspects of creating *Wicked* from conception to finished show.

The Wicked Channel
https://www.youtube.com/watch?v=DncrfElcb-o.

A YouTube channel devoted to the musical *Wicked* featuring thousands of videos covering every aspect of the show.

Bibliography

"An Interview with Gregory Maguire." BookBrowse. Accessed September 30, 2017. https://www.bookbrowse. com/author_interviews/full/index.cfm/author_ number/1051/gregory-maguire.

Baldock, Lee. "Tony Meola's Wicked Wizardry on Broadway." LSiOnline, October 23, 2003. https://www.lsionline.com/ news/tony-meola-s-wicked-wizadry-on-broadway--oxbq4d.

Brantley, Ben. "There's Trouble in Emerald City." *New York Times*, October 31, 2003. http://www.nytimes. com/2003/10/31/movies/theater-review-there-s-trouble-in-emerald-city.html.

Buckley, Michael. "STAGE TO SCREENS: A Chat with Wicked Nominee and TV Veteran Winnie Holzman." *Playbill*, June 6, 2004. http://www.playbill.com/article/ stage-to-screens-a-chat-with-wicked-nominee-and-tv-veteran-winnie-holzman-com-120120.

Fallon, Kevin. "A 'Wicked' Decade: How a Critically Trashed Musical Became a Long-Running Smash." *Daily Beast*, October 31, 2013. https://www.thedailybeast. com/a-wicked-decade-how-a-critically-trashed-musical-became-a-long-running-smash.

"Full Bio." StephenSchwartz.com, accessed October 12, 2017. http://www.stephenschwartz.com/about/full-bio.

Gans, Andrew. "Wicked Breaks Box-Office Record and Remains Broadway's Highest-Grossing Production." *Playbill*, January 3, 2013. http://www.playbill.com/article/wicked-breaks-box-office-record-and-remains-broadways-highest-grossing-production-com-201145.

Gioia, Michael. "The Story Behind the 'Defying Gravity' Music Video Everyone's Talking About and What Wicked's Composer Thought." *Playbill*. October 21, 2015. http://www.playbill.com/article/the-story-behind-the-defying-gravity-music-video-everyones-talking-about-and-what-wickeds-composer-thought-com-368251.

Isherwood, Charles. "It's Still Popular Being Green." *New York Times,* August 21, 2014. https://www.nytimes.com/2014/08/22/theater/a-decade-later-wicked-continues-to-be-catnip-for-tweens.html.

Isherwood, Charles. "Wicked." *Variety*. October 30, 2003. http://variety.com/2003/legit/reviews/wicked-7-1200538236.

"John Bucchino and the origins of *Wicked* the Broadway musical." MusicalSchwartz.com. Accessed October 2, 2017. http://www.musicalschwartz.com/recordings/bucchino.htm.

Long, Jessie. "8 Differences between the Wizard of Oz Movie and Book." LetterPile. May 11, 2016. https://letterpile.com/books/8-Differences-Between-the-Wizard-of-OZ-Movie-and-Book.

Maguire, Gregory. *Wicked: The Life and Times of the Wicked Witch of the West*. New York, NY: HarperCollins, 2007.

Mitchel, Alex. "Mr. Wicked." *New York Times*, March 11, 2007. http://www.nytimes.com/2007/03/11/magazine/11maguire.t.html?mcubz=1.

Nachman, Gerald. *Showstoppers!: The Surprising Backstage Stories of Broadway's Most Remarkable Songs.* Chicago: Chicago Review Press, 2017.

Rawson, Christopher. "Carnegie Mellon University's Stephen Schwartz, 7 others join Theater Hall of Fame." *Pittsburgh Post-Gazette*, January 27, 2010. http://www.post-gazette.com/ae/theater-dance/2010/01/27/Carnegie-Mellon-University-s-Stephen-Schwartz-7-others-join-Theater-Hall-of-Fame/stories/201001270207.

Reside, Doug and David Maxine. "Musical of the Month: A Production History of the 1903 Oz." New York Public Library, December 15, 2011. https://www.nypl.org/blog/2011/12/15/musical-month-production-history-1903-oz.

Sebesta, Judith. "Interview with Stephen Schwartz." *Ecumenica: Journal of Theatre and Performance*, February 16, 2016. http://www.ecumenicajournal.org/ interview-with-stephen-schwartz-2.

Schama, Chloe. "Frank Baum, the Man Behind the Curtain." *Smithsonian*, June 25, 2009. https://www. smithsonianmag.com/arts-culture/frank-baum-the-man-behind-the-curtain-32476330.

Schwartz, Evan I. *Finding Oz: How L. Frank Baum Discovered the Great American Story*. New York: Houghton Mifflin, 2009.

"Stephen Schwartz - Broadway, Film, and Opera Composer and Lyricist." MusicalSchwartz.com, accessed October 5, 2017. http://www.musicalschwartz.com/schwartz.htm.

"Stephen Schwartz." Masterworks Broadway. Accessed October 12, 2017. http://www.masterworksbroadway. com/artist/stephen-schwartz.

Vine, Hannah. "31 Longest Running Broadway Shows." *Playbill*, January 4, 2017. http://www.playbill.com/ article/31-longest-running-broadway-shows.

———. "The 29 Top-Grossing Broadway Shows of All Time." *Playbill*, August 27, 2017. http://www.playbill.com/ article/the-29-top-grossing-broadway-shows-of-all-time.

"Wicked." Internet Broadway Database, accessed October 18, 2017. https://www.ibdb.com/broadway-production/wicked-13485.

"Wicked (2019)." IMDB, accessed October 26, 2017. http://www.imdb.com/title/tt1262426.

"Wicked on Review." BroadwayWorld, October 30, 2003. https://www.broadwayworld.com/reviews/Wicked.

Wootton, Dan. "NIC'S A WICKED GIRL Former X Factor judge Nicole Scherzinger set to land high-profile role of Elphaba in film adaptation of Wicked." *Sun,* April 21, 2017. https://www.thesun.co.uk/tvandshowbiz/3385682/nicole-scherzinger-set-to-land-high-profile-role-of-elphaba-in-film-adaptation-of-wicked.

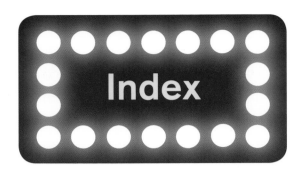

Index

Page numbers in **boldface** are illustrations.

acoustic, 76–77
alto, 75
anime, 76

Baum, L. Frank, 5–6, 9–15, 17, 22, 56, 63, 76
bombastic, 70
book, 10, 18, 21, 29, 31–32, 55, 63
Boq, 50–51, 54

Chenoweth, Kristin, 32–33, **33**, 36, 54, 63, 65, 80
Clock of the Time Dragon, The, **40**, 41, 59
costumes, 41, **42**, 43, 55–58, 57, 60, 65, 70

definitive, 60
"Defying Gravity," 49, 54, 74–77
denizens, 56
Drama Desk Awards, the, 27, 31, 55

Dr. Dillamond, 23, 47–50, 54, 60

Edwardian, 56
Elphaba, **4**, 5–9, 18, 24–25, 29, 33, 36, 38–39, 41, **44**, 45–51, **48**, 54, 58, 60, 62, 65, 67, **68**, 71, 74–78, 80–81

Fiyero, 24, 43, 47–51, 54, 77
flown, 41
frozen, 62

Galinda/Glinda, 7, 14, 24, 32–33, 45–52, **48**, 54, 63, 65, 67, **68**, 75–76, 78, 80
genre, 36
Gershwin Theatre, the, 6, 54, 60, **61**, 66, 74, 81–82
grimmerie, 49–51, 58

hapless, 78
Hilferty, Susan, 41, 55–56, 60
Holzman, Winnie, 10, 18, 21, 24–25, 29–34, **31**, 38–39, 43, 53, 55, 60, 66, 80

iconic, 9
impeccable, 65
infringe, 14, 52

Lee, Eugene, 40–41, 55, 60
leitmotif, 28

Madame Morrible, 7, 43,
    46–51, 54
Maguire, Gregory, 5–6, 8–11,
    13, 17–18, **20**, 21–25, 35–38,
    41, 45, 64, 69, 76, 78, 82
Mantello, Joe, 10, 35–36, **37**,
    38–39, 41, 53, 55, 60, 62
Menzel, Idina, 36, 54–55,
    62–63, **64**, 65, 71, 75–76,
    80–81
movie version, 17–19, 79–82
myriad, 52

Nessarose, 7, 25, 43, 46, 48,
    50–51, 53–54

out-of-town tryout, 39, 43,
    52–53, **52**, 60
Oz the Great and Powerful, 14, **16**

parody, 14, 76
Platt, Marc, 17–19, 21, 24–25,
    32, 34–35, 38, 41, 43, 53,
    79–80, 82
protagonists, 74

rapturous, 63
readings, 33–35, 64
revisionist, 10, 14

sarcastic, 75
Schwartz, Stephen, 10, 17–19,
    17, 21–27, **23**, 29, 32,
    34–39, 43, 53, 55–56, 60,
    62, 64–65, 71, 75–77, 79–82
sentient, 7, 23, 47
sequels, 64, 78–79, **79**
set design, 38–39, **40**, 41, 43,
    55, 70
Stone, David, 34–35, 38–39,
    43, 53, 62, 80, 82
storyboarding, 25, **28**

Tony Awards, the, 11, 27, 31,
    33, 55, 63, **64**

vocal range, 75

*Wicked: The Life and Times
    of the Wicked Witch of the
    West* (source book), 5–7, **8**,
    17–18, 21–25, 32–33, 37–38,
    41, 45, 53, 64, 69, 76, 78
Wiz, The, 11, 14, **15**
Wizard, the, 6–7, 9, 14–15, 17,
    23, 38, 41, 47–51, 60, 75, 78
Wizard of Oz, The (movie), 11,
    14, 24, 29, 33, 52–53, 64,
    66, 69
Wizard of Oz, The (stage
    musical), 11
Wonderful Wizard of Oz, The,
    5–6, 9–13, **13**, 14, 18, 22
workshops, 32, 34, 36

About the Author

JERI FREEDMAN has a Bachelor of Arts degree from Harvard University. She is the past director of Boston Playwrights' Lab, an organization that produced original plays in Boston, Massachusetts. Her play *Uncle Duncan's Delusion* was published by Baker's Plays (now part of Samuel French), and her play *Choices*, co-written with Samuel Bernstein, was staged at the American Theatre of Actors in New York City. She is also the author of more than fifty young-adult nonfiction books, including *Exploring Theater: Stage Management in the Theater* and *Exploring Theater: Directing in the Theater*.